WHO'S SICK TODAY?

by Lynne Cherry

E. P. DUTTON · NEW YORK

This book is dedicated to
Nancy and David Dougherty, Nancy Drye and Bob Thomas,
Gloria and Walt Hallagan, Ellen Calmus, Jim Huffman
and the house on Rosedale Road.

Published in the United States by
E. P. Dutton, a division of
Penguin Books USA Inc.

Published simultaneously in Canada by
Fitzhenry & Whiteside Limited, Toronto

Designer: Riki Levinson

Printed in Hong Kong by South China Printing Co.
First Edition COBE 10 9 8 7 6 5 4 3

Library of Congress Cataloging-in-Publication Data

Cherry, Lynne.
  Who's sick today?/by Lynne Cherry.—1st ed.
    p. cm.
  Summary: Rhyming text and illustrations introduce a
variety of animals with different ailments.
  ISBN 0-525-44380-0
  [1. Sick—Fiction. 2. Animals—Fiction.
3. Stories in rhyme.] I. Title.
PZ8.3.C427Wh 1988   87-22185
[E]—dc19   CIP
                                                          AC

Who's sick today?

Beavers with fevers,

a snake with an ache,

a small red fox with chicken pox.

Who's at the doctor today?

A whale on a scale,

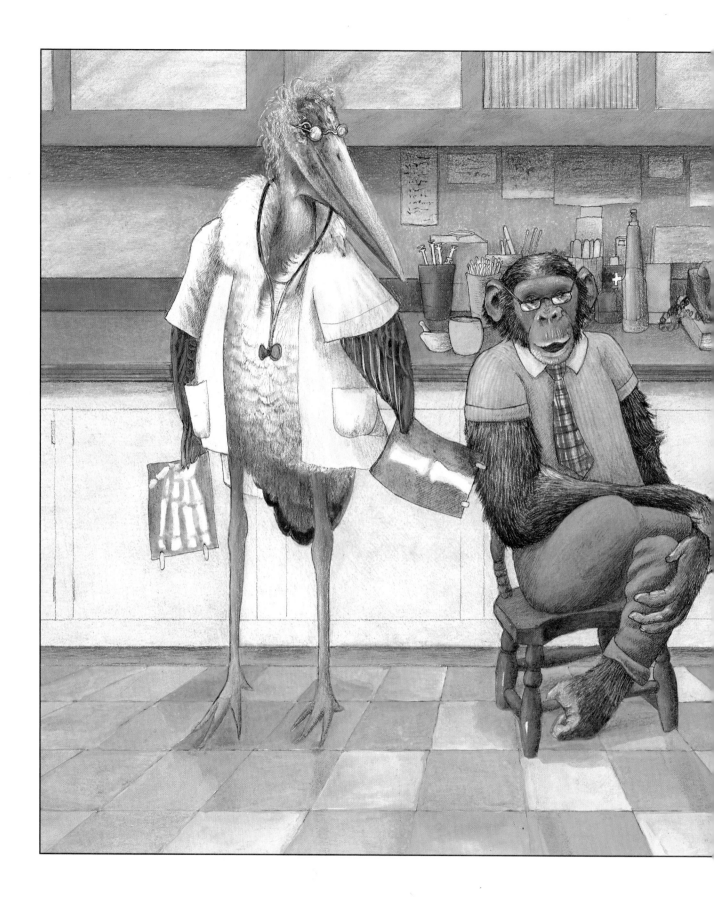

a chimp with a limp,

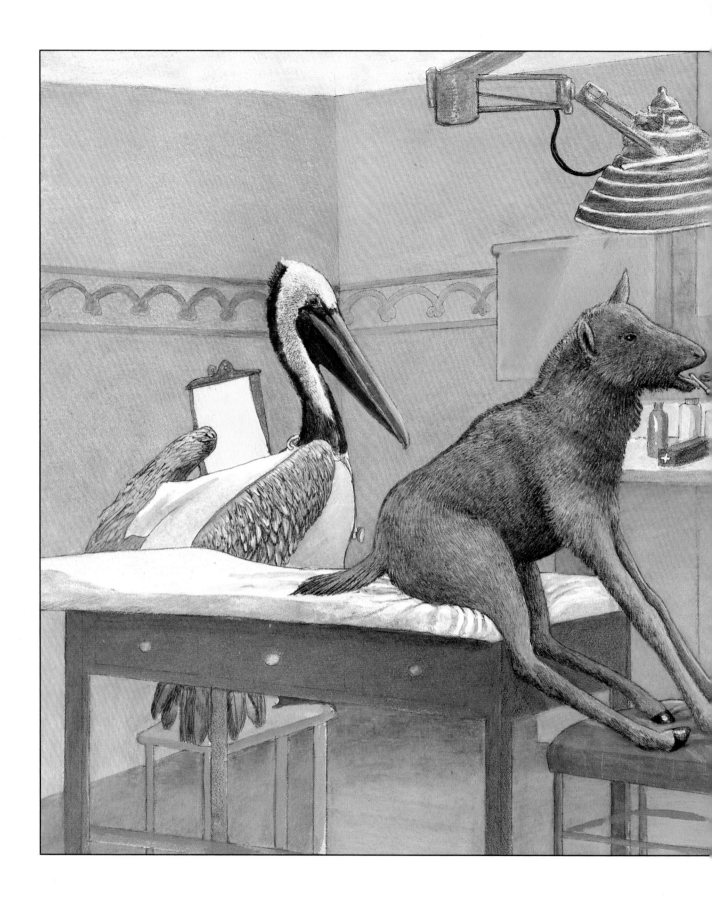

a gnu with the flu.

Who's in the hospital today?

Llamas in pajamas,

young stoats with sore throats,

cranes with pains,

possums with blossoms,

and baboons with balloons.

Who's all better today?
A porcupine who's feeling fine!